is here!

Discover how Plog, a monster with
revoltingly smelly feet, becomes one of
the bravest, most ingenious slime-slingers
in Trashland – a whiffy but wonderful
rubbish dump at the edge of the world.

It's time to fight crime with slime!

Collect all the cool cards and check out
the special website for more slimy stuff:

www.slimesquad.co.uk

Don't miss the rest of the series:

THE SLIME SQUAD VS THE TOXIC TEETH

And coming soon:

THE SLIME SQUAD VS THE CYBER-POOS

THE SLIME SQUAD VS THE SUPERNATURAL SQUIDS

Also available, these fantastic series:

COWS IN ACTION

ASTROSAURS

ASTROSAURS ACADEMY

www.stevecolebooks.co.uk

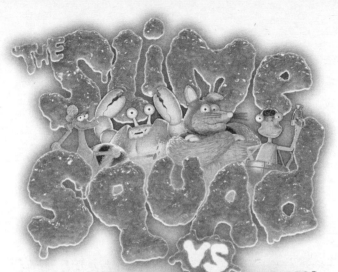

THE SLIME SQUAD

vs

THE FEARSOME FISTS

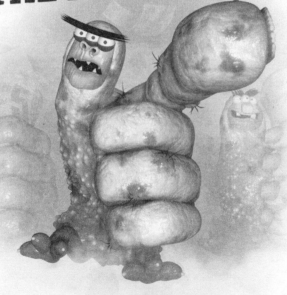

by Steve Cole

Illustrated by Woody Fox

RED FOX

THE SLIME SQUAD vs THE FEARSOME FISTS
A RED FOX BOOK 9781862308763

First published in Great Britain by Red Fox,
an imprint of Random House Children's Books
A Random House Group Company

This edition published 2010

1 3 5 7 9 10 8 6 4 2

Copyright © Steve Cole, 2010
Cover illustration and cards © Andy Parker, 2010
Map © Steve Cole and Dynamo Design, 2010
Illustrations copyright © Woody Fox, 2010

The Random House Group Limited supports the Forest Stewardship
Council (FSC), the leading international forest certification
organization. All our titles that are printed on Greenpeace-approved
FSC-certified paper carry the FSC logo. Our paper procurement policy
can be found at www.rbooks.co.uk/environment.

Mixed Sources
Product group from well-managed
forests and other controlled sources
www.fsc.org Cert no. TT-COC-2139
© 1996 Forest Stewardship Council

Set in 16/20pt Bembo Schoolbook by
Falcon Oast Graphic Art Ltd

Red Fox Books are published by Random House Children's Books,
61–63 Uxbridge Road, London W5 5SA

www.kidsatrandomhouse.co.uk
www.rbooks.co.uk

Addresses for companies within The Random House Group Limited can
be found at: www.randomhouse.co.uk/offices.htm

THE RANDOM HOUSE GROUP Limited Reg. No. 954009

A CIP catalogue record for this book is available from
the British Library.

Printed in the UK by CPI Bookmarque, Croydon CR0 4TD

For Tobey

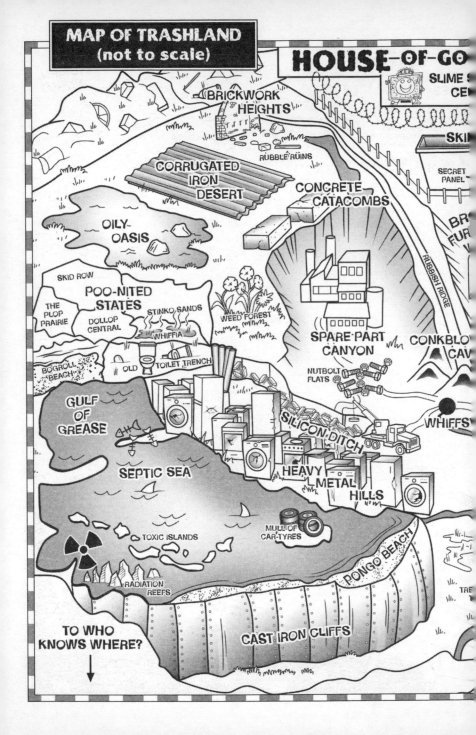

ONCE UPON A SLIME...

The old rubbish dump was a long way from anywhere. It stretched out as far as the eye could see – a mucky, dusty, smelly, rusty landscape of thousands of thrown-away things.

It had been closed for years. Abandoned. Forgotten.

Nobody ever came here. Few people even knew it existed. So there was no one around to wonder who had built the slightly crooked house beside the rubbish dump – or to ask why they had moved away again in such a hurry. There was no one around at all.

Apart from . . . the MONSTERS!

There were thousands of them living here. Millions, maybe. Bright and bold and curious creatures no bigger than a finger, who did not think of the old rubbish dump as a rubbish dump at all.

To them it was a whole wide and wonderful world of whiffy possibilities. They called it *Trashland*.

These miniature monsters didn't know where they had come from. They didn't know *what* they had come from, and they certainly didn't know why.

But they knew that now they were here, they wanted to make the most of it.

So with knowledge they found in thrown-away human books, they got busy inventing the things they needed. They built villages, towns and cities. They worked hard at monster jobs and played hard at monster hobbies.

As the years went by, Trashland became a bustling, happy place where the little monsters lived in peace and where crime was almost unheard of.

And then, one day . . .

Chapter One
A SHAGGY PLOG STORY

Plog the monster woke up in his soggy shoebox home. Sunlight streamed through a big crack in the sewer pipe where the shoebox had washed up long ago. It looked like a lovely morning.

Plog stretched and yawned and thought: *What shall I do today?*

"Same as every day," he mumbled, climbing out of bed.

"I'll watch smellyvision on my own till it's time to go to sleep again."

Scratching his bottom, Plog splashed through the puddles on the floor towards the smellyvision set. He was quite big by miniature monster standards – an orange, bear-shaped animal with a rat-like snout, extra-long ears, a furry tail, tangled whiskers, stripy pyjama bottoms and a grubby brown waistcoat. They were the only clothes Plog owned. But since he never went further than the sewer pipe and no one ever came to visit, it didn't really matter.

"I wish I could go out and make friends and have some fun. I'm fed up with being stuck down here on my own." Plog glanced down at his feet, and shuddered. "But if the ordinary monsters found out my terrible secret, they'd laugh and shout and call me names and drive me out of town . . ."

Just as Plog reached the smellyvision set, his stomach rumbled noisily. *ROARRRR! Blub-bub-bub-GRRRRRRR.* He sighed. He couldn't afford proper food because he didn't have a job. Instead, he ate whatever meals he could put together from stuff he found in the broken sewer pipe — mostly rat hairs and flies' legs in seagull-poo sauce, which tasted pretty horrid but at least stopped his tum from rumbling.

"I'd better go out and find some breakfast," Plog muttered, pushing open his soggy cardboard door and wading into the cold, whiffy water.

A little way down the sewer pipe he found a squashed bit of earthworm. He didn't really fancy that, so he pressed on. A mosquito's wings stuck out temptingly from the scummy water, but again he splashed onwards, enjoying the feel of the sunlight that shone through the cracks in the concrete onto his hairy face.

With a thrill he realized he was nearly at the end of the pipe. It led to the rusty foothills of the Tin Can Mountains – an area of great natural beauty with its gigantic, teetering piles of dented drink containers. Sometimes Plog came here in secret to watch the native spongy monsters go about their business. Cautiously, he peered out . . . and saw a quivering old lady monster. He recognized her wrinkled purple face and enormous bottom. "That's Mrs Bumflop," he murmured with a frown. "Funny, her pet ant's not with her. She normally takes him everywhere . . ."

"Help!" Mrs Bumflop wailed suddenly. "Oh, help! Help, help, help, help, help, help, HELP! Help, help, help. HELLLLLLLLLP!"

Sounds like she needs help, thought Plog, gulping hard.

There was no one else around to answer her cries. Did he dare step out and ask the old dear what was wrong? It was obviously important, and Plog had always wanted to do something brave and helpful – to be a true hero just like the monsters he looked up to most ...

His idols were called Furp, Zill and Danjo. Better known as – the Slime Squad.

These extraordinary characters had special slimy powers and were famous all over Trashland. Very few monsters had useful slime or the skill to handle it well, so the Squad was rarely out of the news. And Plog had filled dozens of scrapbooks with pictures and write-ups of their exploits. Whenever a 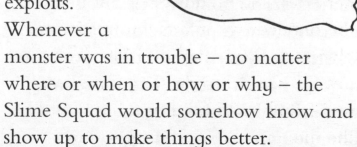 monster was in trouble – no matter where or when or how or why – the Slime Squad would somehow know and show up to make things better.

"HELLLLLLLLLLLLLLLPPPPP!"
wailed Mrs Bumflop, her arms waving
wildly in the air.
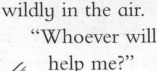
"Whoever will
help me?"
"*I* will!"
Plog
whispered,
his fur wet
with sweat,
willing
himself to
overcome his
fear and step
outside into plain
sight. "*I* will, *I* will—"
"HELP IS AT HAND, MADAM!"
came a croak from on high. And the
next moment, a pale yellow frog-thing –
wearing oversized metal underpants and
a golden crash helmet with a spinning
radar dish poking out of the top –
bounded up with a clatter.

8

Plog's jaw dropped so far it bounced off the bottom of the sewer pipe. "No way . . ." he breathed. "It *can't* be!"

But somehow, incredibly, it *was*.

"Let fear disappear," the frog-monster declared. "The Slime Squad is here!"

Chapter Two
SLIME TIME!

"Ooooh!" squealed Mrs Bumflop who, like Plog, was staring at the half-dressed frog-monster in shock and surprise. "It's *you*! I've seen your picture in the newspoopers!"

The frog-thing smiled modestly. "How lovely for you."

"Furp LeBurp!" Plog boggled in disbelief. "The Slime Squad's sticky-skinned, big-brained high-jumper.

10

He's quite often first on the scene . . ."

"Please, Mr Furp, sir!" Mrs Bumflop was in a flap, running about with her bottom wibbling. "My ant needs saving. He climbed up that can over there and fell in. It's full of rainwater, and he can't swim – not without armbands, anyway!"

"Allow me to hop into action, madam." Suddenly Furp leaped halfway up the side of the can – and used his sensationally slimy hands and feet to stick to its sheer sides. Squelching quietly, he climbed onto the top, peered down through the drinking hole and turned behind him. "Zill!" he called. "Are you there?"

"Oh, mega-wow!" breathed Plog, his heart beating about a billion times a second. "Zill Billie is here too! Right in front of my eyes! In the furry flesh!"

A black-and-white she-monster bounded up to the can; her thick tail wagged, her golden leotard sparkled in the sunlight. She looked like a six-legged skunk crossed with a cool poodle. Three tufts of hair grew from her head like big sprigs of cauliflower, and her eyes were a dazzling mouldy-bean green.

"Hey, Furp. Hey, old lady monster." Zill put four paws on her hips. "What's the emergency?"

"A stuck ant," Furp called back.

"His name is LF, Miss Zill," added Mrs Bumflop.

"LF Ant? Did he come with a trunk?" Zill joked. "Don't worry, we'll get him out." She opened her dainty jaws wide and coughed. *Ka-THWIPP!* A thick string of slime shot out from her mouth and stuck to the top of the can!

Biting the end off with her teeth, she used it as a rope to climb up and join Furp.

"Hey, LF!" she shouted, staring down into the darkness. "Lifeline on its way – grab hold!"

She spat another slimy strand, like super-stretched bubblegum, and dangled it down into the depths. "It's no good, Furp," she said a few seconds later. "The ant is struggling in the water – he can't grab hold of my slime-line."

"Sounds like he needs a helping hand, then!" boomed a deep, cheery voice as a large crimson crab-monster loomed into view on three stocky legs, his golden shorts gleaming. "Or a friendly pincer, anyway!"

"It's Danjo Jigg!" Plog gawped, and for a moment he thought he might faint with excitement. "The biggest, toughest Slime Squaddie of all!"

14

"Danjo, can you make a hole in the side of this can?" Furp shouted down.

"Big enough to let out the water," Zill added, "but small enough to stop the ant being swept away with it?"

"*Tin*-can do!" Danjo replied. He opened his left pincer and a thin jet of sizzling red slime squirted out – burning a small hole at the base of the rusty can. Filthy water came pouring out.

"There! If the ant grabs hold of your slime-line now, Zill, he'll be fine."

"Come on, LF," Zill urged the ant. "You can do it . . . *YES!* Attaboy!"

"You mean, *Ant*aboy!" joked Danjo.

"How brilliant it must be when you're a hero," Plog murmured, watching from his hiding place in the sewer pipe, spellbound. "If only *my* slime was good for helping people. But all it does is cause trouble."

Plog watched as Zill hauled up the slimy rope to reveal a bedraggled ant hanging onto the end. Furp tenderly tucked the soggy insect down the back of his metal underwear. "I'll take LF from here." He climbed back down the side of the can. "And I don't want to hear any jokes about ants in my pants!"

When he reached the
ground Mrs Bumflop
jumped for joy and
scooped up her
bedraggled pet. Danjo
pointed his right
pincer in the air and
squirted ultra-cold
blue slime at the top
of the can, which soon
froze to make an icy slime-slide. Zill
skated down it and jumped elegantly
into Danjo's arms, beaming as the old
lady monster danced with her ant.

A crowd of purple creatures was
starting to gather round.
Not wanting to be
seen, Plog ducked
back into the shadows
of his old sewer pipe
and splashed towards
his shoebox, still
smiling in amazement.

"This is the happiest moment of my life," he declared. "I can't believe I've actually seen a real live Slime Squad rescue with my own eyes! Thank goodness I didn't try to help Mrs Bumflop and make a doofus of myself . . ." Then he stopped and sighed. "If only the Slime Squad could help *me*. If only *anyone* could."

"Hey, you!" A prim female voice echoed around the sewer pipe behind him.

Plog gulped. It sounded like Zill.

"You, the big orange furball with the snout," she went on.

She can't mean me, Plog thought in a daze.

18

"You, the big orange furball called Plog who was watching us rescue that ant just now," she continued.

Slowly, shakily, Plog turned round. Furp, Zill and Danjo were standing a short way away. They were watching him closely.

"That's him all right." Danjo nodded. "Those ears, that tum, that fur on his bum . . . He's our monster."

"You must come with us at once, Plog," said Furp. "Yes, at once." He nodded gravely. "Apparently – unlikely as it might seem – *you* are needed to save the world!"

Chapter Three
TERROR IN THE TUNNELS

"Me? Save the world?" Plog laughed nervously. "Very funny."

Furp looked at Danjo and Zill. "I'm afraid he doesn't believe us."

"I can't really blame him," said Zill. "*I* don't believe us!"

"The PIE wouldn't lie," Danjo said mysteriously.

"But how can I save anything?" Plog shrugged.

"You're the Slime Squad – saving stuff is *your* job. Like the way you rescued that ant."

"We were sent here to find *you*, Fur-boy," said Zill. "It's just lucky for the ant and his owner that we were passing by when we did."

"What you all did out there was amazing." Plog forgot his own troubles as he relived the exciting rescue in his mind. "It was even cooler than the time you helped that woodlouse out of the squashed fizz-bottle."

"Oh!" Zill smiled and fluffed up her sprigs of hair. "You saw that, huh?"

"I've seen *all* your rescues!" Plog enthused. "I've watched them on the smellyvision and read about them in the newspoopers. I must be your biggest fan!

But what I can't understand is how you guys always manage to show up whenever there's trouble."

"We have a very wise friend who points us in the right direction," said Furp, tapping his helmet. "The same friend who told us to bring you back to our hidden base . . ."

"You want to take me to the Slime Squad's HQ?" Plog gulped – *how cool would that be!* But then fear rushed through him. He looked down at his feet, safely hidden in the scummy water, and sighed. If he left the sewer, his awful secret would be revealed. "Sorry. I have to stay here."

"You don't," said Furp, puzzled. "There are no doors, no fences, no walls—"

Plog held up his hairy paws. "Look, I just can't come with you, OK?"

"Sure you can, Fur-boy. It's easy." Zill winked at him. "Danjo will carry you!"

"You betcha." The crab-monster grinned. "My sweet slimy pincers are quite the convincers! Come on, big fella. Let's hustle."

"No, please!" Plog started to struggle as Danjo took hold of his furry armpits. "You don't understand . . ."

But already Danjo's powerful pincers were hauling him clear of the smelly water . . . to reveal

Plog's feet – in all their horrible glory.

They were the largest, hairiest, ugliest feet that any of the Slime Squad had ever seen.

Danjo gasped. Zill's tail stood on end. The radar dish on top of Furp's helmet stopped spinning and blew a fuse.

Here were feet that could break mirrors. Tootsies that would turn the stomach of a concrete cockroach.

"Put me down," groaned Plog, his furry cheeks glowing nuclear-red with shame. "My feet have to be kept wet, or else . . ."

Danjo gasped louder. Furp shrank into his pants and Zill reared up on her back legs as putrid, neon-yellow slime began to ooze from Plog's feet. Faster and faster it came, dripping down into the water in fat splodges.

"Ugh!" Zill's long nose was twitching like it might jump off her face in protest. "That pong would knock the trunk off an elephant."

"It would choke an atomic racoon!" Furp agreed.

"Not to mention a cute crimson crab-monster." Danjo dropped Plog with a splash and staggered back, holding his nose with both pincers.

Feeling horribly ashamed, Plog turned and ran away from the Slime Squad, down into the darkness of the sewer.

"Wait!" called Furp. "Come back!"

But Plog kept running. His luminous foot-slime lit the way as he splashed deeper and deeper into the darkness – until a terrifying, throaty squeal ahead made him skid to a stop. Hot, foul-smelling breath blasted into his face . . .

Looking up, he found a giant snuffling, sharp-toothed monster towering over him! Its fur was wet and dark. Its whiskers were wiry and tangled, and its tail coiled and flexed like a giant pink serpent. The creature's eyes glinted hungrily as it stared down at the furry orange snack-on-legs.

Oh, no, thought Plog, frozen stiff with terror. *A sewer rat!* He had glimpsed such nightmare animals before but never up close. *Even great big human giants are scared of rats – what chance do I have?*

The creature raised a terrible paw to crush him. Acting on pure instinct, Plog batted it aside with a swipe of his tail and bellowed at the animal.

It squealed again, baring its chisel-like teeth – but Plog kicked up his feet and flicked smelly slime into its face and eyes. Spitting and spluttering, shaking its furry head, the rat backed away through a hole in the sewer-pipe wall and vanished from sight.

Panting for breath, Plog stared at the hole for any sign of a twitching nose or a wet whisker. But nothing appeared. Slowly he realized that the hole was in the shape of a giant fist – and that there was a huge, dirty handprint on the wall beside it. *What could have made that?* he wondered.

Then, suddenly, Furp, Zill and Danjo appeared from behind him. "Are you OK, Fur-boy?" Zill looked around warily. "That sounded like a rat."

"It was," said Plog, in a daze. "I . . . I think I scared it off."

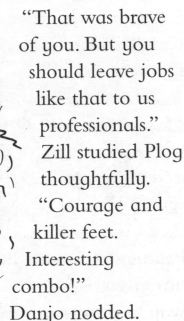

"That was brave of you. But you should leave jobs like that to us professionals." Zill studied Plog thoughtfully. "Courage and killer feet. Interesting combo!"

Danjo nodded. "Don't get me wrong, fella, I'm all for slime – but you've got some seriously toxic foot-action going on there."

"That's why my family kicked me out and sent me away to live down here all on my own," Plog confessed. "Only cold water stops my feet oozing like a slug with the runs, and only sewage can hide the smell."

"Er . . . did you ever think of wearing shoes?" asked Zill.

"I can't. My slime just overflows and . . ." Plog shuddered. "Let's just say it's not good."

The radar dish on Furp's head began to revolve again, and a sly smile spread over his face. "Well, I do believe that brute has given us a way to transport you out of here without undue smelly sliminess." He pointed to two large squishy dollops on the ground.

"Rat droppings! Simply bury your feet in them, and Danjo will freeze them solid." The frog-monster chuckled, setting his metal pants rattling. "Yes, frozen dung ought to keep your feet harmless for a while . . ."

Plog shook his head, astounded. *I've watched my all-time heroes in action, survived a life-and-death battle with a giant killer rat, and now I've got to step into a pair of poo-shoes because the Slime Squad's "friend" thinks I can save the world.* The ghost of a grin crept onto his face. *Looks like it's going to be one of those days!*

Chapter Four

BEHOLD...THE PIE!

Once Plog's feet were frozen into their rat-poo cocoons, Furp, Zill and Danjo led him quickly out of the sewer and into the quiet foothills of the Tin Can Mountains. *I'm outside!* Plog thought. His feet were numb with cold but the rest of him fizzed with excitement. *For the first time in years, I'm out and about . . .*

The stale air smelled beautiful, and the sunlight felt good on his fur as they headed towards a large pale-green haze hovering in the air like a cloud of tiny flies.

"What's that?" Plog asked.

"That's the extremely cunning smokescreen – or should I say *slime*screen – that surrounds our transport," Furp explained. "I made it myself by mixing Zill and Danjo's slime with a pot of whitewash. Whatever you paint with it turns almost invisible!" He grinned. "There's just *so* much you can do with good quality slime!"

Zill nodded. "The slimescreen means that no one can follow the Slime-mobile to our hidden base."

"But it also means we sometimes forget where we parked!" added Danjo.

Furp hopped up on top of the faint green swirl and seemed to hover in mid-air. He pressed a button on the side of his pants, and with a loud *clunk*, an invisible door swished open. "All aboard!"

Eyes wide with wonder, Plog was bundled into a green-and-white vehicle as big as a bus. The front was crammed with complicated controls like the cockpit of a plane, and big pedals stuck out from the floor. There was also a massive steering wheel with three seats arranged around it.

Above this was a large tinted windscreen; heavy shutters slid back to reveal the tin can landscape outside. Battered control units lined both sides like rusting sentries. To the rear of the Slime-mobile the space was dominated by a large dirty toilet surrounded by desks that were smothered in bottles and beakers, brimful of unknown potions in a dozen indescribable colours.

"Oh, wow," Plog breathed. "C-c-c-cool!"

"I see you've spotted my lav-lab," said Furp proudly.

"Part lavatory, part laboratory – the perfect spot for slimy experiments."

"Save the science stuff for later . . ." Zill fluffed up her tail, sank into the driver's seat and grinned over at Plog. "Wanna see what this baby can do, Furboy?" Before he could reply, she hit a big red button. "Yeee-haaaaaa!"

With a sudden rev of engines and an almighty lurch, the Slime-mobile powered away at unbelievable speed. *Vr-vrr-VROOOOOM!* Plog was thrown to the floor with a yelp. His tummy spun one way and his head whirled another. *Good job I skipped breakfast,* he thought.

Furp hopped into the toilet and Danjo leaped onto a chair, riding it as though it were a surfboard.

"Go-go-GO!" he yelled, his three legs holding him as steady as a tripod.

Plog closed his eyes tightly as the Slime-mobile went faster and faster. And when he opened them, he wished he hadn't. The sheer metal wall of a giant yellow skip was looming up ahead. They were zooming towards it on a collision course! "Brake!" he yelled. "Start braking!"

"Relax, Fur-boy!" Zill told him. At the last possible second, a door opened in the side of the skip. "We hang out in a hidden base, remember?"

The Slime-mobile whizzed through the hole and into a dark tunnel. Then Zill stamped on a pedal with three of

her paws and the
Slime-mobile screeched
to a stop. "We're here!"
she announced.

"Splendid!" Furp
jumped out of the lav
and Danjo hopped
down from his chair.

Fear and excitement
mixed in Plog's furry
belly as Zill, Danjo and Furp led him
from the secret garage into a dark
underground passage. He caught a
glimmer of light ahead,
a shining crack in
the blackness. As he
approached it, the
crack grew wider:
a secret door was
swinging open . . .

"Welcome to
our base," said
Furp proudly.

Plog stared around a whopping rectangular room. Everything was so big! A colossal light bulb burned like a sun below a solid sky of peeling plaster. Huge desks lay upturned on the filthy floor, half buried under crumpled papers and broken bottles, while the white walls were daubed with numbers and symbols that Plog didn't understand.

But his attention was quickly drawn to a gigantic battered computer, towering in the middle of the room. Wires and circuits spilled from its cracked casing like fabulous jewellery. To Plog, the glowing white line that flickered and wibbled across the green monitor looked a little like a mighty mouth, while the two dots that danced above it were almost like eyes . . .

"Welcome, Plog!" boomed a deep robotic voice as the line wiggled further and the dots swelled in size. "I am the All-Seeing PIE."

Plog would have jumped if his feet hadn't been weighed down with iced rat-poo. "You, er . . ." He swallowed hard. "You don't look much like a pie to me."

"I'm not a real pie, obviously!" the computer retorted a little tetchily. "PIE is short for Perfect Intelligent Electronics. I am a super-advanced self-operating computer system."

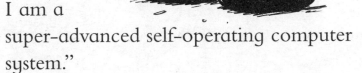

"PIE watches over all Trashland," Furp whispered.

"He's our boss," Zill added. "He brought us together, a whole year ago now. We were just ordinary monsters . . ."

40

"But I saw how kind and clever and determined you were – and how SLIMY – and knew how *extraordinary* you could be as a team!" PIE remembered fondly.

Furp nodded. "He sent each of us a top secret wee-mail summoning us to this base—"

"So we could start up the Slime Squad," Danjo concluded. "To do good deeds and help monsters in need."

"And the monsters of Trashland have never needed help more than they do now," boomed PIE.

"What do you mean?" Plog asked quietly. "And what's it got to do with me?"

PIE's dots and lines
grew wobblier. "Have
you never wondered
how life in Trashland
began, Plog? Have
you never thought of
the human giants whose
world we share – and
wondered why they stay
away? Have you never
wondered why the fluff in your
bellybutton is always blue?"

Plog blinked. "Not really."

"I KNOW THE ANSWERS, PLOG!"
the computer cried urgently. "Well, apart
from that bellybutton thing. But I know
too that a dark and deadly danger
threatens our world." PIE's voice dropped
to a grating whisper. "Do you desire my
knowledge, Plog? Do you dare to learn
the truth? Will you allow your life to
change for ever in ways you could never
have foreseen? For, once I begin my tale,

there can be no going back . . ."

Plog gulped. "Not even if I need the toilet?"

"Well . . ." PIE considered. "You could perhaps pop back to the lav-lab for a quick wee-break if necessary."

"What if he needs a poo?" wondered Danjo.

Furp nodded. "Or, indeed, a wee *and* a poo."

"I'll hold it in," Plog declared boldly. He glanced down at his frozen feet, looked up at his heroes and then stared in wonder at their computerized boss. "I *want* my life to change for ever. All-Seeing PIE – tell me your tale!"

Chapter Five

LIFE, TRASHLAND AND EVERYTHING

Plog waited for PIE to speak, his heart in his mouth. "Well?"

"I was leaving a dramatic pause," said PIE indignantly.

"Sorry," said Plog. "Only Furp said something crazy about me being needed to save Trashland."

"It is not crazy," PIE snapped. "It is very, very serious. But before we get on to *saving* Trashland, I must tell you the secret of how it was created."

44

"Wow," breathed Plog and Danjo.

Furp gasped in wonder. "You mean you actually know?"

"Huh!" Zill folded four of her arms and shot Plog a resentful look. "Me and Furp and Danjo have been helping monsters for a year, and you've never told us. How come Fur-boy gets the gossip the moment you slap eyes on him?"

"I don't have eyes," PIE boomed. "I have sensors. And as I told you, my sensors have detected a deadly danger gathering around Trashland that threatens everything we have ever worked for: the happiness of the little monster, wherever he or she may be!"

PIE's circuits were almost popping with passion. "The three of you have done marvellous monster work throughout Trashland, but you have never faced EVIL before. None of us have. Alas! All that is about to change . . ."

"I see," Zill murmured. "Sorry."

Plog swallowed hard and waited for PIE to explain further.

"In the beginning," boomed the computer, "there was rubbish. Tons and tons of rubbish piled high on a landfill site – a landfill site that was closed down in mysterious circumstances. Then a human being came along—"

"I've seen those human giants in books," said Furp.

"They look so weird." Danjo shivered. "They give me the creeps."

"Without this particular human, none of you would have existed," PIE told them primly. "Indeed, this secret base is actually the cellar of the house that he built here."

Plog's fur stood on end. "*What?*"

"Godfrey Gunk was a great scientist," PIE explained. "He was very worried about the increasing amounts of pollution and rubbish in the world. His dream was to create marvellous mutant mini-monsters out of chemical goo – monsters who would clean up the planet by eating, drinking and generally devouring all types of trash.

So Godfrey bought an old closed landfill site, built a lab beside it and got to work."

"How come you know so much about him?" asked Plog.

PIE's screen dimmed. "Because I was once his faithful super-computer. His greatest invention. I worked with him to make his dreams come true. Of course, he wanted to make good, friendly, peaceful monsters who would be no trouble to look after, so he was very careful to keep the nastiest, stinkiest, most toxic waste separate from the rest. He worked and toiled, and experimented, and slaved, and invented, and toiled some more, and experimented harder for years and years, and . . ."

"And?" Furp urged him eagerly.

"And got precisely nowhere," PIE concluded. "In the end, penniless and miserable, Godfrey became a *mad* scientist. He threw the hissiest hissy-fit ever, smashed me open and hurled my audio-visual components to the four corners of the tip."

Plog winced. "Sounds awful."

"Actually, it turned out to be a good thing," PIE revealed. "I was programmed with powers of self-repair, and found I could still see and hear through my scattered circuits – wherever they'd ended up – thanks to my wonderful wireless connections."

Danjo smiled with understanding. "So *that's* how you became the All-Seeing PIE."

"And how you watch out for everybody to this day," said Zill.

"But if Godfrey's experiments got nowhere, how did we monsters appear on the scene?" asked Furp. "Where did we come from?"

PIE resumed his explanation. "Godfrey wrecked his lab, chucked all his experiments out of the window and moved away, never to return . . . But what he didn't know was that the dump had been closed with good reason. Years before, piles of top-secret radioactive waste was accidentally buried here. And within a few weeks of Godfrey's going, its potent powers kick-started an incredible chemical reaction. Life began to form. Amazing mini-monsters sprang up with incredible speed . . ."

"And Trashland was born," breathed Furp.

"Cool!" chorused the others.

"Trashland has always been a peaceful place," PIE went on. "But recently the radiation finally reacted with the contents of a lead-lined box in the furthest, darkest corner of the rubbish dump 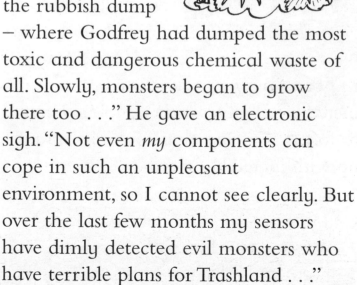 – where Godfrey had dumped the most toxic and dangerous chemical waste of all. Slowly, monsters began to grow there too . . ." He gave an electronic sigh. "Not even *my* components can cope in such an unpleasant environment, so I cannot see clearly. But over the last few months my sensors have dimly detected evil monsters who have terrible plans for Trashland . . ."

Danjo looked baffled. "You mean, they'll do *really* bad things . . . on purpose?"

"I believe so," PIE said gravely. "I fear that these evil monsters will steal and fight and rob and hurt and attack anyone or anything they choose."

"That's horrible!" Zill cried.

"I know," said PIE. "Which is why you must stop them!"

"But . . . we can't stand up to monsters like that," Furp protested.

Danjo nodded. "We help nice monsters in trouble. We scare off rats and pigeons. We save helpless ants."

"We've never had to *battle* anyone," Zill agreed.

"You can do it!" said Plog. "You guys are the Slime Squad – you can deal with anything!"

"Of course they can . . ." PIE paused. "Provided *you* join them."

"*WHAT?*" spluttered Plog. "But . . . but . . . but . . ."

His words trailed off. There was a long, uncomfortable and slightly smelly silence.

"So this stuff about Fur-boy saving the world," said Zill with icy calmness. "It involves him *joining* the Slime Squad?"

"But it's always been just the three of us," Danjo protested.

Furp scratched his crash helmet. "PIE knows best, I suppose."

"But I'll be no use to you guys," said Plog. "I'm rubbish! I've spent the last few years hiding in a sewer!"

"My sensors indicate that if Plog does *not* join the Slime Squad, the world will fall into chaos and destruction . . ." Suddenly an alarm sounded – *A-WOWW, WOWW, WOWW!* – and a flashing red light appeared on PIE's cracked screen. "An armed robbery is in progress at a rank bank in Broken Furniture Valley."

"What's an arm ribbery?" Furp
wondered.

"*Armed robbery*," PIE corrected him. "It
means that evil monsters are using
weapons to take something that doesn't
belong to them. You must stop them –
all four of you."

Furp swapped
uneasy looks
with Zill and
Danjo.

As for Plog,
his heart was
flapping about
in his chest like
a bird going
bonkers. He
was scared and excited and reeling
with all PIE had said. But if there was
a chance to help his idols – and to help
himself – he knew he had to take it.
"I'll try my best not to mess up," he said
quietly. "And I'll do whatever you say."

Zill sighed. "Then you'd better come with us to the Slime-mobile."

"Right." Danjo clenched his pincers and nodded. "'Cos when danger looms large, the Slime Squad cry *CHARGE!*"

And, bellowing "*Charge!*" at the tops of their voices, the four monsters jumped, thumped and galloped into action – and into the unknown . . .

Chapter Six
FIST ATTACK!

Within seconds, the Slime-mobile was rocketing away from the secret base and onto the rubbishy roads of Trashland. Zill steered towards the Broken Furniture Valley.

"I've just had an awful thought," she announced.

Furp nodded. "We're about to fight EVIL MONSTERS!"

"Almost as bad . . ." said Zill. "The Slime Squad has a fourth member – without a matching outfit!"

Danjo reached into a box beside his seat. "I've got a spare pair of gold shorts you could wear, Plog."

Plog looked at the shorts doubtfully. "They look a bit small."

"Then wear them on your head," Zill snapped. "If you're going to join us, you have to make an effort."

Feeling a bit silly, Plog squeezed the shorts onto his head and pulled his long ears through the leg holes. As he did so, his nose twitched. He realized that his frozen toes were starting to thaw – which meant that his feet were starting to pong.

Furp had noticed too. "I have an idea," he said quickly, hopping over to the lav-lab and pointing to two iron cauldrons. "I use these for boiling up slime for my experiments – stick your feet in them and you can wear them like shoes!"

"OK," Plog said uncertainly. He squashed his feet into them. It was a tight fit.

Furp used his crash helmet to scoop up water from the toilet bowl and ladle it into the makeshift shoes. "That should keep your slime under control!"

Plog was about to thank him when Zill called out: "We're almost there. Oh! What is that—"

Ker-BANG! PANG! KROOOOM!

The Slime-mobile crumpled and crunched with the impact. Jets of safety-slime splooshed out from the steering wheel over the four monsters, hardening like rubber to protect them as the windscreen shattered. Plog bounced around helplessly like a giant pinball, yelling in alarm – until the vehicle stopped rocking, the slime melted away and he fell trembling to the floor. Thick green smoke poured from the Slime-mobile's damaged controls, hiding the others from view.

"Zill? Furp? Danjo?" Plog said anxiously. "Call out and I'll help you . . ."

"Ooof!" came Zill's muffled voice below him. "You can stop standing on my tail for a start!"

"Sorry." Plog stooped to help her up – just as Furp hopped out of the smoke in front of them, his metal pants dented and his crash helmet askew.

"I can't understand it!" the frog-monster cried. "The Slime-mobile's anti-crash sensors have never let us down before. Whatever did we hit?"

"And where's Danjo?" Plog asked – then spotted a tall dark shape looming out of the smoke ahead of him. "Phew! He's there."

"That's not me," said Danjo groggily just behind them. "I'm here!"

"So who is that?" Zill muttered as the shape came closer.

"They must've got in through the windscreen." Furp gulped. "Er, we're terribly sorry for smashing into you—"

"You didn't," came a rough, snarling voice. "Our mega-missile smashed into *you!*"

Suddenly the smoke cleared to reveal the weirdest monster Plog had ever seen. It looked like a massive fist, waddling on four tiny feet. The fist-monster's skin was hard and chapped, covered in warts and blisters. Its thick thumb looked like a giant serpent, with three evil-looking eyes staring out from the nail above a dribbling nose and a mean little split for a mouth.

62

"I'm Knuckles," the monster growled.
"Leader of the Fearsome Fists." Two
more hulking fist-creatures stepped up
behind him, looking – if possible – even
rougher. "This is Palmer and Nail.
They're my deputies."

"Pleased to meet you," said Furp
nervously. "We're the Slime
Squad – er, and Plog.
What's a missile?"

"A high-speed weapon invented by
us," Knuckles said. "You've seen what we
can do. So stay out of our way – or
we'll make you pay."

"Hey! I do the rhymes!" Danjo
complained.

But Knuckles and his deputies had already turned and lumbered back out through the broken windscreen.

"Well," said Furp. "Perhaps we should do as he says and clear off."

"No way." Plog scowled. "He can't talk to you like that!"

"He just did," Furp pointed out.

"Fur-boy's right," said Zill. "Those creeps just totalled our transport. We can't let them get away with it."

Danjo nodded. "Let's go to work on the thumb-faced jerks!"

Plog tried walking towards the doors. *CLANK! CLANK!* The cauldrons on

 his feet weighed a ton. He peered out through the clearing smoke to find a crowd of frightened monsters watching *six* of the fist-creatures

further down the road. The Fists were
running in and out of the smashed-in
window of the rank bank. A black van
was parked nearby with a strange
contraption strapped to its roof.

"That must be their missile launcher,"
Furp twittered.

But Plog was more interested in
what the Fists were doing: they were
stuffing banknotes into the back of their
van. Monster money was printed on
used toilet paper – the smellier the note,
the more valuable it was. And from the
stink of things, these Fists were stealing
a fortune.

"Look at me!" Knuckles laughed, clutching a bundle of soggy five-pong notes. "A bunch of fives with a bunch of fives!"

"Stop!" Plog cried, staggering out of the Slime-mobile. "That money doesn't belong to you!"

Knuckles smiled while his friends continued their work. "What are you going to do – tell my mummy?"

A wrinkly fist-monster with grey hair peered out of the van. "Huh? Tell me what?"

"Shut up, Mum!" Knuckles snapped.

"That's no way to talk to your mother, fist-face," Danjo said, jumping down from the crumpled Slime-mobile and pointing a pincer. "Even if she *is* a big dumb crooked monster like you."

Zill and Furp hopped into sight too.

"Yay, it's the Slime Squad!" cheered one watching monster.

"They'll take care of these baddies," said another.

"But who's the big furry one with buckets on his feet and shorts on his head?" said the first one.

"He's as big a loser as all the others," jeered Knuckles. With a sudden surge of speed he charged at Plog and punched him hard.

"*Oof!*" Plog flew backwards and smashed into Danjo – just as Danjo tried to fire a blast of steaming slime from his hot pincer.

The sizzling stream struck Furp instead, full in the face!

"*Urp!*" Furp spluttered, wiping slime from his eyes as his crash helmet started to smoke.

He glimpsed Nail lumbering towards him and tried to hop clear — accidentally whacking Plog in the face with his steel pants before a slap from Palmer sent him flying into the screaming crowd.

"I'll get you for that," Danjo growled at Palmer, raising his cold pincer. But Nail smashed a nearby fire hydrant and sewer water spurted out at super-fast speed. Danjo froze up the water as it surged towards him — but he couldn't stop it, and wound up buried under a mini-mountain of slimy ice.

"That does it!" Now Zill was galloping into the fray. "Prepare to be slimed!"

"No, Zill!" Plog warned her dizzily. "He's too tough to tackle alone!"

"We'll see about *that*." Zill shot out a slime-line at Knuckles – but he simply caught it in his gruesome grip and tugged on it hard. Zill found herself reeled in like a struggling six-legged stripy poodle-fish, straight into a sucker-punch from Palmer. "*Ow!*"

Plog struggled up and tried to catch her as she flew by – but she was moving so fast that the impact knocked him clear out of his cauldron boots!

They both went down hard, skidding across the ground and flattening Furp just as he'd crawled clear of the crowd.

"This is a disaster," Zill groaned. "We can't stop them!"

Plog watched helplessly as Knuckles, Nail and Palmer thumped closer. *My first misson with the Slime Squad,* he thought. *And it looks like it'll be my last!*

Chapter Seven

STINK OUT AND WALK OUT

"Come on, lads, we're all done here!"
Knuckles' mum shouted, cramming the
last notes into the van and slamming
the door. "Pinkie, Forefinger, get in
here." Two Fists — one with a red nose
and one with extra-long fingers —
hopped into the vehicle. "Knuckles, Nail,
Palmer — let's be
having you!"

Knuckles
glared at Plog,
Zill and Furp —
then turned to his
mum and nodded.
"All right," he snarled.

"This lot won't be giving us any more trouble. Let's move out." Palmer and Nail bounced back into the van after him.

"They're getting away!" wailed a monster in the crowd.

"We've got to stop them," said Plog desperately. But then, with horror, he saw that his bare feet were oozing slime, and the terrible smell was already filling the air. "Oh, no!" he cried, searching for his cauldrons.

"*Ugh!*" The crowd recoiled, clutching their noses.

Suddenly Plog heard the Fists' van start up with a rattling roar.

Furp and Zill tried to run after it but slipped in Plog's foot-slime and crashed to the ground.

"*Arggh!*" Zill cried. "That stinky stuff's all over my fur!"

Furp cringed. "It's even in my pants!"

"Sorry." Plog was trying to squeeze his feet into his makeshift boots. "I'm so sorry."

Danjo crawled out of the ice pile, battered and bedraggled, while Furp and Zill clung onto each other, struggling to stand upright in the stinky soup. Plog's feet finally squeezed into the cauldrons with a disgusting *squelch*. Meanwhile the Fists screeched away in their van, leaving behind only a cloud of dust and the smell of banknotes. The Slime Squad stared after them, stunned, slimy and helpless.

"You were rubbish!" a big monster yelled from the shocked crowd. "Useless!"

"So much for the Slime Squad," said a young red blob. "To think I used to look up to you!"

A pale quaking monster in a pinstripe suit came out of the rank bank. "You let them take everyone's money!" He stared at the squad. "How could you?"

The crowd began to jeer and boo. Plog's cheeks burned redder than a nuclear strawberry. Zill ran back to the Slime-mobile with tears in her eyes.

Heads hung low, Furp and Danjo
followed her.

Last of all was Plog – his head in his
hands, his feet in iron buckets, and his
hopes and dreams in tatters.

It took the Slime Squad ages to return
to the hidden HQ. The Slime-mobile
had been badly damaged by the
fist-monsters' missile and could only go
slowly. Shaken and sad, no one said a
word the whole journey back. Plog
stood miserably in the lav-lab, his feet
out of harm's way in the toilet's cold,
scummy water.

Zill parked the Slime-mobile in the secret underground garage. Then she, Furp and Danjo trooped outside. Plog forced his troublesome feet back into the cauldrons and clanked along after the others.

The All-Seeing PIE's cracked screen was fizzing with red lights and exclamation marks of every size. "Well," he boomed, "that didn't go very well, did it?"

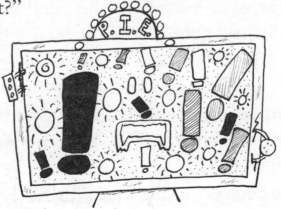

"I'm sorry I messed up," Plog said quietly.

"We *all* messed up," sighed Danjo.

Furp nodded. "We went to pieces."

"Those horrid Fists." Zill shuddered.

"They're almost as revolting as Fur-boy's feet."

"And we were booed." Danjo closed his eyes. "The whole experience was rotten."

"But the *really* rotten thing is that loads of monsters lost their money," Plog said. "The Fists took it and we couldn't stop them."

"No one can stop those things," Zill declared.

"At least only a few people saw us fail," said Danjo.

"Afraid not," said PIE. "The three o'clock poos had a reporter there with a camera. All Trashland has seen his report . . ."

Plog, Zill, Furp and Danjo stared in horror as PIE played the pictures on his screen. There were the four of them, slipping, tumbling and getting walloped. The reporter's voice cut in: "*From the moment they emerged from their still-smoking Slime-mobile, the Slime Squad's members were largely useless — even with the addition of a mysterious fourth monster in a strange costume who kept getting in everyone's way. Already monsters all over Trashland are asking — has the Slime Squad had its day?*"

Plog looked away as the crowds on the screen began to boo, unable to watch any more.

"So that's what we get for risking our necks and trying to help!" Zill stormed, her eyes full of tears.

"Well, if people think we're finished –
fine. I quit!"

"Me too," said Danjo hotly.

Furp nodded.
"Someone else
can deal with
those fist-things
next time."

"But" – Plog
looked at them –
"there *is* no one
else. You can't quit! Tell them, PIE."

"I cannot tell anyone to risk their
lives if they don't want to," PIE replied.

"I'm sure PIE will find some
replacements for us," said Furp. "He's
already found you, Plog. Perhaps you
can all save the world together."

"But you *can't* go!" Plog implored the
frog-monster. "None of you can. We
were so surprised today, we forgot the
most important thing: the Slime Squad
is a *team*. We only failed because we

tried to tackle them one by one, without a plan."

"Uh-uh, Fur-boy," growled Zill. "*We* got nowhere because *your* dumb slimy feet made us slip about so much we couldn't even stand!"

"That's not fair." Plog was stung. "It was *you* who knocked me out of my boots!"

"The two of you nearly squished me," Furp huffed. "And as for Danjo squirting me in the face—"

"That was Plog's fault," Danjo protested. "He jogged my pincer."

"What a lot of moaners!" Zill complained.

But then PIE cut across their bickering. "WARNING!" he warbled.

"My sensors have sighted the Fearsome Fists heading for the Goo York area. I believe they are going to rob another rank bank!"

Plog gasped. "So soon after the last one?"

"Even if the Slime-mobile was working," said Furp, "we wouldn't be able to stop them."

"That's right," said Zill. "Oh, well. I . . . I wanted to spend more time watching smellyvision anyway." She blew her nose noisily. "That's just fine . . ."

"Oh, Zill," Plog sighed.

Danjo sniffed. "I'll make myself useful by fixing the Slime-mobile – for the next guys who want to use it."

Plog shook his head sadly. "You *can't* give up, Danjo. Please?"

Danjo hesitated for a moment. Then he slowly trudged away on his three legs.

"Furp?" Plog looked at him hopefully.

"Er, you can keep the cauldrons, my dear Plog. But I've been meaning to make more time for my experiments in any case." The frog-monster nodded to himself. "There really is so much you can do with mixed-up slime . . ."

"PIE," Plog begged, "stop them, please!"

"All must find their own way," said PIE mysteriously.

"Yeah, to the exit," Zill agreed.

"But you three have always been my heroes!" Plog insisted. "You can't just give up when something goes wrong!"

"Well, *you* did!" Zill shot back.

Plog opened his mouth to reply, but realized she was right. He'd let his fear of his foul feet spoil his life and send him scuttling underground. "But you're better than me," he whispered. "Tell them, PIE."

But PIE remained silent.

Alone now in the hidden HQ, Plog pulled the golden shorts off his head, carefully folded them, and placed them inside his waistcoat. Then he clanked off to begin the long journey home.

Chapter Eight
PLOG IN DANGER

Plog took his time on the way back
to his sewer. He didn't like the idea of
returning to the dank darkness, so he
made the journey last several days. It
was nice outside. The rubbish was
pleasantly smelly and there
weren't many monsters
about.

His golden shorts sparkled in the sunlight through his threadbare waistcoat. At night he used them as a pillow. Every time he fell asleep, he woke up hoping that the fight with the Fists had been just a bad dream, and that the Slime Squad was still together.

Sadly, the dreadful events of that afternoon had been all too real.

And the Fists were growing bolder. On the second day of his long walk Plog had found a discarded newspooper reporting that the Fists had robbed five more rank banks, leaving a trail of terror across the land. And on the third day he'd overheard a radio bulletin: confident that nobody would dare to challenge them, the Fists had robbed a terrifying total of *twelve* rank banks in as many hours. It was getting so that decent, law-abiding monsters were scared to go out on the streets.

So that's why it's so deserted around here, Plog thought with a shiver. It was a shiver that grew ever shiverier as he remembered the newsreader's closing comments: "*No one knows why the Fearsome Fists are robbing quite so many rank banks. No one has seen them buy anything. But their getaway vehicle has been spotted most commonly in the area of the Tin Can Mountains . . .*"

"Where I live!" Plog breathed. Looking around, he realized he had reached the rusty outskirts of the district. And suddenly he remembered the giant handprint on the wall of his sewer, and the huge hole he had found there. It could only have been made by the Fists! But those clues had been left *before* the robberies had begun. What did it all mean?

Plog's thoughts were interrupted by a piercing scream from behind a nearby stack of cans. "Sounds like Mrs Bumflop," he muttered. "She must be in trouble again!"

He quickened his step, old tin crumpling under his metal boots. Then he was thrown to the ground by an explosion somewhere close by. Black smoke belched out into the air and several giant cans toppled over, rolling down the rusty slope like unstoppable steamrollers – straight towards Plog!

He scrambled up, just barely dodging them — and the golden shorts fell out of his waistcoat.

Without really thinking, Plog pulled them on over his head. He heard the scream again. *It doesn't matter if I can't save the world*, he thought, breaking into a run. *I'll settle for saving Mrs Bumflop . . . or anyone else in trouble.*

But as Plog pounded round the corner past an extra-large can, he felt his blood start to freeze. Knuckles and his Fearsome Fists had blown up the rank bank closest to Plog's home in the sewers, and were seizing wads of filthy banknotes in their fat sweaty fingers. Mrs Bumflop had dropped her startled ant and Nail was holding her round the waist. "Stop your caterwauling," he growled, "or I'll squeeze you like a stuffed prune!"

"Let her go!" Plog shouted angrily.

At the sound of his barked command, Nail jumped in surprise. Knuckles turned, and the other blistered, blotchy Fists looked up with grim and gruesome expressions.

Plog gulped, but knew he couldn't stop now. "You heard me," he went on with a wobble in his voice. "Let her go, *now*!"

Nail's mouth twisted into a leer. "Who's going to make me?"

"I will!" Plog yelled. He picked up an old ring-pull and flicked it through the air. To his amazement, it stayed right on course and caught Nail bang on the knuckles – breaking his hold on Mrs Bumflop.

"Run!" Plog told his old neighbour, scooping up her ant and plonking it in her arms. "Hide in your house and don't come out."

"Good advice," snarled Knuckles, lumbering closer as the grateful monster-madam fled for her life. "Shame you didn't take it yourself."

"We don't like nosy parkers sticking their snouts in," growled Palmer. He paused. "Or do I mean snouty parkers sticking their noses in?"

"Whichever way, we don't like it," croaked Pinkie, the Fist with the runny red nose.

"Actually, we don't like anything!" added Forefinger, his long-fingered friend.

"Well, I don't like you robbing all these rank banks," said Plog. "So why don't you give back the money and push off!"

"We don't take notice of anyone but Lord Klukk," growled Knuckles.

"Lord who? Is he your boss?" Plog folded his arms. "Well, you just tell him that if he keeps sending you lot to rob rank banks he's going to be in a whole heap of trouble!"

"I've got a better idea," Knuckles rumbled. "Why don't you tell him *yourself*?"

Suddenly, out of the corner of his eye, Plog caught movement. He whirled round to find Knuckles' mum sneaking up behind him. *BAM!* She dived forward and Plog was struck by a half-ton of wrinkled, warty flesh. The world spun like a Catherine wheel through his head and he crashed to the ground . . .

When Plog's senses switched on again, he found himself in the clutches of the Fearsome Fists. He was being dragged through a damp, dark and strangely familiar tunnel by Pinkie and Palmer. *This is my sewer!* he realized in a daze. *Maybe Knuckles and his gang aren't so bad — they're taking me home!*

But the Fists passed Plog's forlorn, soggy shoebox without a second glance and hauled him further into the shadows.

With an icy pang of fear, Plog recognized the large, fist-shaped hole in the sewer wall as he was bundled through it into the space beyond.

Properly awake now, he realized that the Slime Squad weren't the only ones with a hidden HQ. This dark concrete cave had to be where the Fists hung out in their spare time. Their van was parked in one corner – it must have driven on ahead, so stuffed full of loot there was no room for passengers. Heavy-duty hammocks hung between sturdy poles so the Fists could catch some shut-eye. Massive stacks of cash had been piled against the walls in whiffy heaps. A battered smellyvision set perched crookedly on top of a pile of rancid rubbish. The whole place was revolting, even by monster standards.

*To think — the Fists were my neighbours
and I never knew it!* Plog scowled. They
had most likely chosen this location for
the same reasons he had: the sewer was
close to civilization, and yet hidden
away from prying eyes. But while Plog
had dreamed of living with normal
monsters, the Fists wanted only to take
from them — and here was the perfect
place from which to whizz out and

cause trouble in
the world outside.

"So, you're
awake," growled
Palmer in Plog's
ear.

"Why have
you brought me
here?" Plog demanded.

Knuckles waddled up, his scuffed,
callused fingers flexing like overstuffed
elephant trunks. "To talk to our boss, of
course."

"Lord Klukk?" said Plog nervously.

Forefinger pressed a big red button on the smellyvision. Immediately the screen started to flash black and red. As Plog watched, a dark shape appeared – the sinister shadow of a large, bird-like creature with a curved, cruel beak and a wobbly bit on top of its head.

"Your lordship?" said Knuckles, and Plog was sure he detected a note of fear in the Fist's gruff voice. "We've got one of your enemies. He was with those slimy idiots who tried to stop us at the rank bank in Broken Furniture Valley."

"Ah, yes," said the figure on the screen in a throaty, half-strangled rasp. "The fool who fought alongside the insufferable Slime Squad. How kind of your friends to stay out of my way."

"That's what you think," Plog retorted. "They – they're planning something that will stop you in your tracks. Just you wait."

"I think I will be waiting for a very long time," Klukk hissed back. "And sadly, your membership of that silly squad will *buk-buk*-be oh-so-very *buk-buk*-brief . . ."

Knuckles smiled. "What do you want us to do, your very important bossiness?"

Lord Klukk rounded on him. "I want

you to send all that lovely looted lolly to my Evil Experiments Lab right away. I need the cash if I am to conquer all Trashland!"

Plog gasped. PIE had been right about the evil monsters wanting to rule the world. "*Why* do you want to conquer Trashland?" he demanded.

"That's for me to know and you to completely fail to find out . . ." Lord Klukk gave a chilling snigger. "All those who oppose 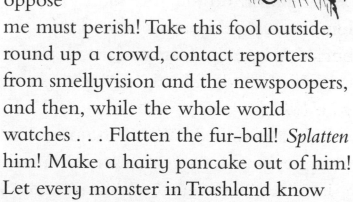 me must perish! Take this fool outside, round up a crowd, contact reporters from smellyvision and the newspoopers, and then, while the whole world watches . . . Flatten the fur-ball! *Splatten* him! Make a hairy pancake out of him! Let every monster in Trashland know the dreadful fate that *buk-buk*-befalls those who dare to stand against me!"

"Brilliant, your super-lordliness!" Knuckles beamed, his blisters glowing red with mirth. "After a show of strength like that, no one will dare to interfere with your plans."

The other Fists laughed too. Plog couldn't believe his long furry ears. "You evil monsters!"

"Yep," Knuckles' mum agreed happily. "Now, you heard the boss, lads – let's take this furry dope outside and deal with him – permanently!"

Chapter Nine

SECONDS FROM SPLATTING!

Plog felt panic rise up inside him as he
was marched back out into the sunlight,
the fat, chapped fingers of Nail and
Palmer locked onto his arms. He knew
he was doomed, but what scared him
even more was knowing that no one
in Trashland could stand up to the full
furious might of
these evil fist-
monsters.
Not now
the Slime
Squad
had given
up . . .

No, he told himself firmly. I'm *not giving up. There must be something I can do . . .*

He racked his brains for ideas as the Fists dragged him through the dented streets of the Tin Can foothills. Ahead of them, Knuckles, Pinkie and Forefinger were hauling monsters from their rusty houses, ordering them to come and see the gruesome "Squash the Plog" show, due to start any time now. Knuckles' mum was on the phone to the monster media, urging them to get their top reporters down here for a story they would never forget . . .

Then Palmer and Nail came to
a halt. Plog watched the frightened
crowds start to form around him, close
to the very spot where
the Slime Squad
had saved Mrs
Bumflop's ant
just a few
days ago.

Once he
would have
felt uncomfortable
with so many strangers staring at him.
But now things had changed. He was
tired of being a victim, stuck alone in
the dark. He *liked* it outside, and he liked
Trashland the way it was. How dare
Lord Klukk and his Fists think they
could ruin everything? He had to get
away and make Zill, Furp and Danjo
see that Lord Klukk – and whatever he
was planning – needed to be stopped.

But how?

"Look at the furry freak," sneered
Forefinger. "Trying to act brave when
he's shaking in his boots."

Plog gasped. BOOTS! *That's it*, he
thought. *The one thing that might just save
me . . .*

Knuckles turned to
the scared-looking
crowd
rounded up
by his hench-
fists, and the
gaggle of
goggle-eyed
reporters
who'd just
sped to the
scene. Plog noticed Mrs Bumflop
cowering helplessly at the back.

"Listen up, you miserable lot!"
Knuckles roared. "This furry orange
bear-rat with the dumb shoes has tried
to mess with our plans not once, but

twice. He has failed! And now our master, Lord Klukk, wants to make it very clear that *anyone* who tries to resist us will *not* live to regret it . . ."

A gasp went up from the crowd. The reporters swapped shocked looks.

"My friend Palmer here is going to climb up one of these cans, jump off and squash this interfering fur-ball flat." Knuckles wore a big grin on his face. "Flatter than a flatfish run over by a steamroller with a nuclear rolling pin."

The crowd gasped again as Palmer starting shinning up a lemonade can, his fearsome fingers piercing the rusty metal as he gripped it. Forefinger took his place holding onto the struggling Plog.

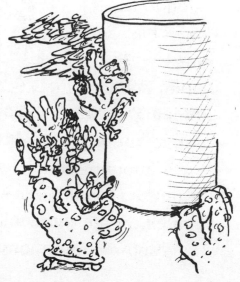

"Watch me!" bellowed Palmer. "I'm gonna leave him as flat as a cannonball."

"A cannonball isn't flat," called one of the reporters.

"IT IS WHEN I'VE FINISHED WITH IT!" Palmer boomed, reaching the top of the tin can. "Stand by for squashing!"

"Wait!" Plog yelled. "Erm, don't I get a last request?"

Knuckles' three eyes narrowed. "No."

"It's an easy one," Plog went on quickly, "and it's really Palmer I'm thinking of. Won't you let me take off these stupid big boots of mine? I wouldn't want him to hurt himself on the sharp edges while he's squishing me into monster paste . . ."

"Aww." Palmer looked pleased. "How thoughtful."

"Very well," Knuckles agreed grudgingly.

Slowly, his heart pounding, Plog prised the iron cauldrons off his feet. The crowd fell deathly silent. Palmer flexed

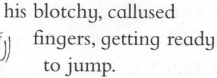

his blotchy, callused fingers, getting ready to jump.

"Come on," Plog hissed to his feet. "Come *on* . . ."

Then, suddenly, the choking, smoking super-stench of Plog's foot-slime was wafting up into the air. Nail and Forefinger staggered backwards and knocked into Pinkie. Knuckles and his mum keeled over, gasping for breath, and the gathered crowds groaned and backed away.

But for once, Plog was delighted with the reaction – especially as Palmer was so busy spluttering and wheezing he lost his balance and toppled from his perch. "ARRRRGH!" He plummeted through the air and landed nails-first on a pile of rusty cans with a splintering *crash*.

"Did it!" Plog cried. He jumped back into his boots and raced away up the nearest rusty hillside, the angry shouts of the Fists clamouring behind him. He picked a path through the cans that towered and tilted all around. If he could only lead Knuckles and his knuckleheads away from the innocent crowd so that no bystanders got hurt . . .

However, Plog was barely halfway up the hill when tough, blistered fingers closed around his legs and brought him crashing to the ground. It was Pinkie, his nose red and running, his mouth twisted into a smirk of satisfaction. "Bad luck for you, I've got a cold," he croaked.

"Can't smell a thing . . ."

Plog tried to pull free, but Pinkie's
grip was unbreakable. He could see
Knuckles and the rest of the Fists
lumbering towards him. *There's no escape
this time*, Plog thought. *I've had it!*

But suddenly a streak of gold, iron
and yellow came whizzing over the top
of the hill. It landed on top of Pinkie,
who got such a fright that he let go of
Plog and jumped in the air.

Plog scrambled up and stared, astounded, at the frog-monster in the metal pants and crash helmet riding the thrashing Fist like it was a bucking bronco. "Furp?!"

"Yes, my dear Plog, it's me!" Furp beamed. "And I didn't come alone . . ."

Plog did a delighted double take as a thick strand of slime shot out from behind a can further up the hill, lassoed Pinkie and spun him round and round. "Zill?!"

"Who else, Fur-boy?" She leaped out from behind another tin and fluttered her eyelashes. "You were doing fine, but we figured you wouldn't mind a little help."

Furp jumped clear as she tugged hard on the slime-line, sending Pinkie spinning off out of control – until a pincer punched out from a nearby can and blasted icy slime at him, freezing him to the spot. Danjo tore his way out of the can and smashed his smaller pincers right into the fist-monster, shattering the ice and knocking the big bruiser flying.

Furp punched the air. "Let fear disappear . . ."

"THE SLIME SQUAD IS HERE!" Zill and Danjo joined in – and so did Plog, his ears standing up proudly through the leg-holes of his golden headgear.

"Not you jokers again?" Knuckles looked at his fellow fist-monsters and laughed. "We took you apart last time we tangled. Don't you know when to give up?"

"We certainly do," Furp informed him. "NEVER!"

"That's what we came by to tell you, Plog," said Danjo excitedly. "You were right. We couldn't just drop out the moment things got tough."

"That would have been way too sensible," Zill agreed wryly. "But you were ready to fight again, Fur-boy, even though you got totally trounced."

Knuckles nodded and smirked. "Twice!"

"But Plog came back fighting," Furp shouted back, "and so have we!"

"Guess we're like you after all, Fur-boy."

Zill grinned at him. "Except obviously my feet are *way* cuter!"

"They won't be when we've finished with them." Knuckles and his fellow Fists stamped forward threateningly. "Even with Pinkie and Palmer in a daze, the four of us can bat you into oblivion!"

"We'll see about that, thumb-face," Plog growled back. "It's time for the final fist-fight – and the winner takes all."

Fury burned in the Fists' fierce little eyes. Then, with a brutish bellowed war cry, Knuckles led his followers in a mad scramble up the rusty slope to get the Slime Squad . . .

Chapter Ten
HERE TO STAY!

As the hard-skinned monsters approached, Zill arched her back and shook her tail. "Don't worry, boys – I'll trip them up with a slime-line!"

"I'll blast them with boiling goo," Danjo said.

Furp bounced onto his shoulder. "And I can't wait to try out my brand-new slimy invention on them!"

"Wait," Plog urged them.

"We charged in blindly before and it got us nowhere." He saw that the curious crowd, led by the newspooper reporters, had followed the Fists up the hill. All eyes were on the Slime Squad. "We need a plan."

Zill shot him a look. "But the Fists are nearly on top of us!"

"Ice-slime, Danjo," Plog cried. "Aim low!"

Danjo pointed his right pincer and a stream of blue slime shot out and hardened over the crumpled-tin hillside. Knuckles and his gang started slipping and sliding back down the hill, smashing onto their backs.

"Good thinking, Plog!" said Danjo happily.

Plog turned to Furp. "Now, quickly – what *is* your invention?"

"Yesterday in the lav-lab I mixed a sample of your foot-goo with slime samples taken from the three of us," Furp said, pulling a handful of strange round capsules from inside his pants. "I got some rather interesting results . . ."

Plog had no idea what the capsules might be, but he trusted Furp completely. "Zill," he said, "can you keep the Fists busy while Furp shows us what this stuff can do?"

"Can I? Ha!" She threw back her poodly snout. "Can a nug-wasp eat nettles with its feet?"

Plog soon learned that the answer was a definite *yes*! As the fist-monsters pushed themselves up again, Zill ran from side to side spitting out not one strand, not two, but a whole cat's-cradle of slime-lines! Intricate as a spider's web, they covered the width of the canyon like gooey tripwires.

"This won't stop us from squashing you!" Knuckles warned her. His blisters grew red with rage as he struggled to shove his way through the sticky strands. "We'll tear you apart!"

"There's a *serious flaw* with that plan." Danjo crouched down, aimed his left pincer under the strands and sent red-hot slime flooding out over the ground. The rusty tin sizzled and smoked, singeing the Fists' little feet. "Or do I mean a *searing-hot floor*?"

"That's got to be the worst joke I've ever heard." Plog smiled grimly as the Fists roared and hopped up and down, tripping over more of the slime-lines and cursing at the tops of their lungs. "And the funniest thing I've ever seen!"

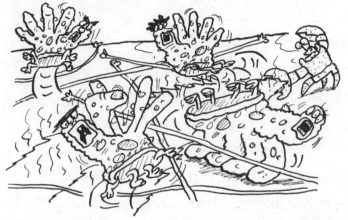

"Wait till you see *this!*" said Furp, who was rolling his round, colourful creations in a little of Danjo's steaming slime. "I've softened the shells – it's time to put my lotion into motion."

"Hey," said Danjo, "I do the rhymes."

"And the four of us make the *slimes!*" Furp's froggy eyes were agleam. "Which means that now I can do . . . THIS!"

He leaped through the air and stuck to the side of a can. Then he threw down one of the balls. It burst over Knuckles, covering his rough, chapped fingers in sticky yellow goop.

"What is that stuff?" cried the Fist. "Get it off! Get it off!"

Knuckles' mum rushed over to obey, wiping the gunk from her son's tough skin. But Furp leaped up and threw another slime-ball as he did so, which coated her in the same mysterious stuff. "Eeuwww!" she warbled. "It's dripping down my back and making me tingle! Someone wipe it away!"

Forefinger and Nail did what they could, but Furp was bombarding them too. And he made especially sure to pelt Palmer, who was staggering across the battered tin battlefield to help up Pinkie.

CRACK! KRESH! Pinkie took a direct hit too. As the balls broke open like eggs, their gooey insides splatted over the fist-monsters' tough, hardened skin.

And went to work . . .

"UGH!" Knuckles groaned. "What's happening to me? My fingers feel all . . . soft!"

"Mine too!" wailed Knuckles' mum. "The cracks in my skin are healing up! I'm losing my wrinkles!"

"Oh, no!" Forefinger stared desperately at his digits. "My blisters are fading!"

"And my warts are going away!" moaned Nail.

"My skin's all pink and fresh!" Knuckles was hopping about in distress. "It feels disgustingly smooth and supple!"

"And so it should!" Furp jumped back down beside Plog, Zill and Danjo. "Because that goo I got onto you is the finest *slimy hand cream* ever invented!"

Plog grinned. "Hand cream?"

"Just a few drops refreshes the skin and leaves it looking youthful and blemish-free," said Furp modestly.

"But . . . but we're big, tough, ugly, hardnut Fists . . ." Knuckles looked like he was about to burst into tears. "You've made us all soft and girly!"

"I'll show you girly," Zill retorted. She galloped up and clobbered him with a four-pawed karate chop, then spun round and socked him in the face with her brushy black-and-white tail.

"*OW!*" Knuckles squealed, tumbling to the ground. "That really hurt!"

Nail and Forefinger charged in to help him. But Plog and Danjo rushed forward, grabbed a big soft thumb each and swung the gang members round and round. *KA-KLACK! OOOF!* The oversized Fists collided and fell to the ground with a clatter.

"Ouch!" Forefinger wriggled on the rusty metal. "That's sharp!"

"I can't bear it!" shrieked Nail, rather melodramatically.

Danjo beamed. "If you can't take the slime, don't do the crime! Not so tough now, are you?"

"Without their blisters, dead skin and calluses, they have no in-built protection," Furp explained, bouncing on top of the other two fist-creeps and hammering them into the ground.

Plog rounded on Pinkie and Palmer. The former thugs were now soft and smooth as a baby's bottom, clinging together for comfort. "Are you ready to give up, or do we have to give you a handshake you will never forget?"

"Noooooo!" Palmer pleaded. "We can't fight you any more."

"We're too sensitive," Pinkie agreed, sniffing noisily.

"We don't stand a chance like this," Knuckles wailed. "We . . . we surrender."

"YAYYYY!" The crowd sent up a huge cheer, which echoed through the rusty foothills as Plog, Zill, Furp and Danjo rounded up the fist-monsters and herded them all together.

"So, here's the deal," Plog told the Fists. "We'll let you push off back to whatever nasty radioactive hole you crawled out of. But you won't be taking any of the money you stole. We're going to give it back to the rank banks."

Another cheer went up from the crowd.

Knuckles narrowed his three eyes. "Lord Klukk will get you for this."

"I think he's more likely to get *you* after the muck-up you've made," Plog retorted. "So when you see him, you can tell him that he'll *never* take over Trashland."

Zill nodded proudly. "Not while the Slime Squad is around."

"Come on, everyone!" cried Mrs Bumflop, her cheeks flushed with excitement. Even her ant was baring its teeth. "Let's drive those horrible Fists out of town."

"*YES!*" The crowd surged forward, their own fists raised – a whole lot smaller, but ready to bruise.

"Gulp!" Forefinger's fingers flew up in alarm. "Time we were off!"

Knuckles hurried his gang away, the whole bunch of them cursing because bits of metal were poking into their sensitive skin.

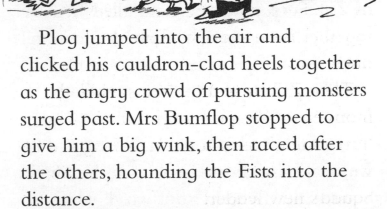

Plog jumped into the air and clicked his cauldron-clad heels together as the angry crowd of pursuing monsters surged past. Mrs Bumflop stopped to give him a big wink, then raced after the others, hounding the Fists into the distance.

Plog smiled and waved – and then
a flock of newspooper reporters came
rushing up, taking pictures and waving
microphones like
lollipops.

"Sensational!"
one said. "What a
comeback! What
a victory!"

"But who's this
furry thing with the
funny mask and
dodgy feet?" said another
monster beside him.

Plog blushed. He watched nervously
as Zill, Furp and Danjo huddled
together for a short whispered
discussion.

Then Zill turned to the assembled
monsters of the press and smiled. "This
'furry thing', as you put it, is Plog – and
we very much hope he will be the Slime
Squad's new leader!"

Plog gasped even louder than the reporters. "What?" He stared at them in astonishment. "But . . . you've already got the All-Seeing PIE."

"He can guide us," said Furp, "but he can't *lead* us into action when he's stuck in our HQ."

"Was it his idea to ask me?" Plog wondered.

"No. It was ours," said Danjo. "PIE knew he couldn't tell us to risk our lives for Trashland. It had to be something we decided to do for ourselves."

"And if it wasn't for you, we might never have done so," said Furp. "That's why PIE said you were needed to save the world. You were needed to take charge of *us*."

Danjo nodded. "You've proved yourself to be the bravest of us all, Plog.

While we were ready to give up, you just carried on."

"And since you know our moves better than we do – and just what we should do with them," Zill continued, "you're the obvious choice to lead us."

"I . . ." Plog scratched his head. "I don't know what to say."

"You wanted your life to change, Fur-boy." Zill's eyes were bright. "So, say yes!"

Everyone looked at Plog. And slowly, very slowly, a delighted smile spread over his face. "All right," he said. "I'm in!"

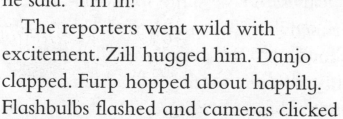

The reporters went wild with excitement. Zill hugged him. Danjo clapped. Furp hopped about happily. Flashbulbs flashed and cameras clicked and newsflashes interrupted all smellyvision programmes, letting the whole of Trashland know of the Slime Squad's incredible victory.

Back in the Squad's hidden headquarters, the All-Seeing, All-*Dancing* PIE laid down some very funky moves, a big yellow smiley face flashing on his screen. "That's my team," he thought proudly.

And in a top-secret, dark and extremely smelly evil lair – beyond the reach of even PIE's spectacular sensors – Lord Klukk crossly scratched the ground with his claws. "Those slimy fools will pay for meddling with my plans," he squawked. "Oh, how they will pay. They will pay by the *buk-buk*-bucket-load!"

"Of course!" A skinny, shadowy, big-beaked servant bowed low and lovingly. "But, er . . . how are *we* going to pay for the next stage of your horrifying master plan? We're skint!"

"Not for long," hissed the sinister monster mastermind. "Relying on the Not-So-Fearsome Fists was foolish. Next time I will choose my evil lackeys with greater care. And when I do, the first thing on my to-do list will be to destroy that sickening Slime Squad!"

But over in the Tin Can Mountains, surrounded by cameras and microphones, Plog and his friends knew nothing of this. They were simply enjoying the

feeling of something new and
momentous beginning for them all.

"Mr Plog," a reporter asked, "as the
Slime Squad's new leader, how do you
feel?"

"Just at this moment," said Plog, "I
feel over the Moon, around the Sun and
all the way back down to Earth again."

Furp, Danjo and Zill smiled as he
raised a furry fist high into the air, and
his head-shorts sparkled in the evening
sunlight. "Bad guys everywhere had
better watch out. The Slime Squad are
back – and we're here to stay!"

DON'T MISS THE SLIME SQUAD'S NEXT INCREDIBLE ADVENTURE . . .

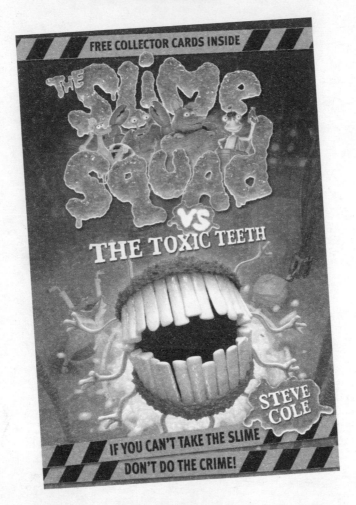

Out now!